ISLINGTON LIBRARIES

D1329020

3 0120 02382182 0

MISS BUBBLE'S TROUBLES
TAMARIND BOOKS 978 1 848 53024 9

Published in Great Britain by Tamarind Books,
a division of Random House Children's Books
A Random House Group Company

This edition published 2010

1 3 5 7 9 10 8 6 4 2

Text copyright © Malaika Rose Stanley, 2010
Illustrations copyright © Jan Smith, 2010

The right of Malaika Rose Stanley and Jan Smith to be identified as
the author and illustrator of this work has been asserted in accordance with
the Copyright, Designs and Patents Act 1988.

All rights reserved. No part of this publication may be reproduced,
stored in a retrieval system, or transmitted in any form or by any means,
electronic, mechanical, photocopying, recording or otherwise, without the
prior permission of the publishers.

TAMARIND BOOKS
61–63 Uxbridge Road, London, W5 5SA

www.tamarindbooks.co.uk
www.kidsatrandomhouse.co.uk
www.rbooks.co.uk

Addresses for companies within The Random House Group Limited can be
found at: www.randomhouse.co.uk/offices.htm
THE RANDOM HOUSE GROUP Limited Reg. No. 954009

A CIP catalogue record for this book is available from the British Library.
Printed in China

Miss Bubble's Troubles

by Malaika Rose Stanley
Illustrated by Jan Smith

Tamarind

For Azizi –
probably the best nephew in the world
M.R.S.

For George, Dennis and Oscar –
the men in my life!
J.S.

Miss Bubble was a teacher
at Topley Primary School,
where she loved all the children
and they thought she was cool.

Miss Bubble's best-known feature was
her splendid head of hair.
She had long, luscious locks
which she styled and wrapped with care.

Miss Bubble lived in Topley town
with a parrot and a cat.
She would have liked a dog as well
but had no room for that.

Her living room was full of books,
her kitchen full of spices.
She loved detective novels
and rum 'n' raisin ices.

At school, Miss Bubble's children
were punctual and proud.
They were hardly ever absent
and almost never loud.

4

Rainbow Class worked really hard
and all of them were keen
to be the most delightful class
Miss B had ever seen.

The children learned times tables.

$$1 \times 6 = 6$$
$$2 \times 6 = 12$$
$$3 \times 6 = 18$$
$$4 \times 6 =$$

They learned to cook and bake.

They learned poetry and astronomy
and how to give and take.

They studied Vikings and Victorians,
French and ICT...

... scientific exploration,

RE and geography.

The class played games and music
and had fun with all their friends.
They made fantastic works of art
from recycled odds and ends.

Mums and Dads were delighted
that their children were so smart.
What a great combination:
busy brain and loving heart!

Miss Bubble told great stories
that could make you cry or laugh.
You could sniffle in a tissue
or split your sides in half.

11

Miss Bubble spent one evening
planning lessons for the week.
She fed her cat, called Milkshake,
and the parrot she called Shriek.

She planned to put her feet up and
watch the *News at Ten*.

She made a cup of cocoa,
got some biscuits and
that's when...
Miss B tripped over Milkshake
as she padded down the hall.
The biscuits flew up off the plate,
the cocoa drenched the wall.

But wait! It wasn't over.
There's a little more to tell.
Shriek dived to catch the falling crumbs...
Miss Bubble dodged and fell.

She did a triple somersault and
landed on her head.

It could have been much worse, of course.
At least she wasn't dead!

Miss Bubble's locks lay tangled,
in a heap upon the floor.
Her pets had never seen her
in such a mess before.

Milkshake grabbed her mobile
and then dialled 999.
Shriek squawked, "Come quick! Come quick!"
down the telephone line.

16

The operator who took the call
tried to calm them down.
A police car and an ambulance
went speeding through town.
When the police came to the door,
Milkshake undid the lock.
"Clever pets," said the paramedic.
Shriek squawked, "What's up doc?"

They rushed Miss B to A & E
with a flashing, bright blue light
and a loudly screaming siren,
which pierced the peaceful night.

Miss B lay on a trolley,
feeling very sick and sad.
A bandage hid her lovely locks.
The diagnosis was bad.
"Who am I?" she said feebly.
"Does anyone know my name?
I don't remember anything
and nothing feels the same."

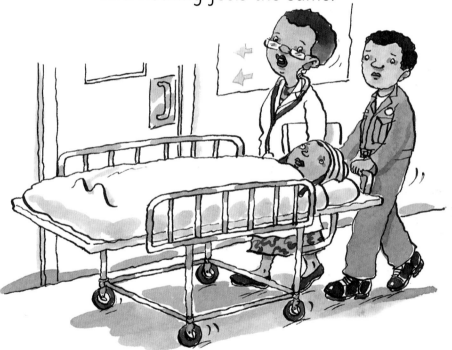

"You banged your head quite badly,"
said the cleverest doctor there.
"We can't give you your memory back,
but will give you our best care."

19

Miss Bubble's friends and family
brought cards and grapes and flowers.
She didn't know who they were
though they sat with her for hours.

Things didn't get any better.
Miss B was badly concussed.
"What now?" asked her sister.
"She can't lie here, gathering dust!"
All the nurses and the doctors
shook their heads and looked away.
They studied their big medical books
but didn't know what to say.

Then Miss Bubble's sister, Petal,
decided what to do.
She knew for sure that Rainbow Class
would have an idea or two.

Matron began to panic.
"It's two visitors per bed!
But now you say
you want to bring
thirty teacher's
pets instead?"

But Sister Petal insisted.
She knew this was the key.
Rainbow Class was sure to jog
Miss Bubble's memory.

So Rainbow Class left
Topley School,

and jumped
onto a bus.

They reached
Miss Bubble's bedside
in a jumble of trouble
and fuss.

Milkshake and Shriek slipped inside
amidst the hustle and bustle.
They hissed and squawked and
scratched the doors but
Miss B moved not a muscle.

Rainbow Class then did their best
to put on a special show
to try and wake Miss Bubble up
and bring back her get-up-and-go.
The girls and boys tried everything
to wake her from her trance.

Rehana played the recorder

and Luke did an Irish dance.

Kwesi was a magician,

Tomasz whirled
his best yo-yo.

Ali and Dwight juggled,

and Grace did karate and judo.

25

Nadira put on a puppet show,

Imran performed
a mime.

Azizi told a story

and Kai recited a rhyme.

Max and Hassan sang a song

and Labaan did
football tricks.

Mia and Jade
whistled a tune.

Cheung did acrobatics.

27

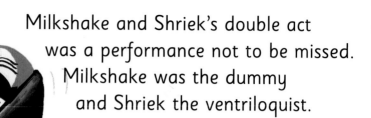

Milkshake and Shriek's double act
was a performance not to be missed.
Milkshake was the dummy
and Shriek the ventriloquist.

Letiya performed a rap,

Demetrius danced ballet.

Leila told some funny
jokes and then...

... the class performed a play.

But when it was all over,
the children got no reward.
Miss B just lay there quietly
and didn't even applaud.

The ward was quiet as a grave.
It seemed that time stood still,
until Miss B opened her eyes
though she still looked a little ill.

Suddenly she sat up in bed!
She smiled, then flashed a grin.
"Hello, Rainbow Class," she said.
"What's all the noise and din?
And why are we hanging around?
We have so much to do.
Doctor, please pass my coat and shoes.
Class, form an orderly queue!"

All the doctors and the nurses
were incredibly amazed.
Sister Petal looked up and whispered,
"Oh, heaven be praised."

The plan to call the children in
had clearly worked a treat.
Miss B was back to normal
and stood on her own two feet.

Shriek flew onto her shoulder,
Milkshake leaped into her arms.
"Thank you all," said Miss Bubble,
"for saving me with your charms."

Rainbow Class jumped for joy and
cheered loudly for Miss Bubble.
Everyone was glad to put
an end to all her trouble.

Miss B then twirled her luscious locks
and checked she looked her best.
Then she rushed the children back to school...
She remembered – they had a test!